Published by Savage Owl Press
Dallas, TX
SavageOwlPress.com

For permissions contact:
permissions@savageowlpress.com

Illustrated by Kindred

Paperback ISBN-13: 979-8-9878454-0-0

* This book contains many highlighted words that children
in the 8-12 year old reading range may be unfamiliar with.
Definitions for these words are provided in the children's
dictionary section in the back of the book for easy reference
while reading.

The R.U.M.P. Chronicles

Thundar the ~~Mighty~~ *Timid*

Copernicus PenDragon

Book One

The White Dragon

Chapter 1

Thundar was a barbarian king of the ancient land of Astoria, and he was frightened. Sure, he was tall and confident. He was brave and noble. He was bold and bright. But sometimes, he was afraid. Actually, Thundar could be many different things on any given day. He suffered from what was called Really Unpredictable Multiple Personalities, or R.U.M.P disorder for short (a term he did not find amusing). One day he could be Thundar the Mighty, defender of the land of Astoria, the next day he could be Thundar the arachnophobic and be deathly afraid of spiders. Such was life for a king with multiple personalities. As if being king of a vast and ancient land was not difficult enough.

Astoria was a great kingdom many years ago, during a long forgotten era of history. It thrived in a time when most modern scholars believed there was no life on earth, at all. Not only *was* there life on earth so long ago, but it was alive with magic, as well.

All over earth, mystical and amazing creatures fought for wealth, power and survival. Trolls, dwarves, witches, wizards and many other fantastic beings made their way through this dangerous world. And of course, there were the barbarians.

Barbarians were taller and stronger than normal humans. They were known for their bravery, intelligence, and a high regard for honor. There were many barbarian kingdoms throughout ancient earth, but none was as peaceful or prosperous as Astoria. While some parts of the world struggled through turmoil, Astoria often remained calm and steady. Although Thundar was often embarrassed by his R.U.M.P disorder, his strong leadership kept trouble at bay and earned the respect of his people.

No one really knew how many personalities Thundar actually had. His servants had given up on keeping track. One of those servants was named Grizby. He was Thundar's most trusted advisor and held the title *Hand of the King*. Grizby once tried to keep a list of Thundar's many characters. He wanted to be ready if *Thundar the Cranky* were to grace them with his presence again. Or perhaps, *Thundar the Dim-witted*. Who could forget a young king Thundar at the annual Astorian Astronomy Gathering excitedly proclaiming that there was a Big Dipper in the front courtyard AND in the back, as well?

"Look everyone! There's another Big Dipper back here!" he shouted in child-like amazement. Distinguished guests from all over the realm snickered among themselves.

Those were days no one wanted to remember; except Grizby. He believed in being prepared.

Some say the list grew so long that an entire room in the castle was devoted to storing it. Grizby only retired the list after he gave up his own bedroom for extra space. Rumors circulated that he actually slept on a cot in the castle dungeon for three whole months!

Each morning, members of Thundar's staff waited nervously to find out who he would be that day. He would roll out of bed and ring his shiny service bell. A flurry of helpers would come in to lay out his clothes and help get him ready for the day. The easy days were ones when he was himself - *Thundar the Mighty*. But on one of those early mornings, the king woke as *Thundar the Timid*. This version of Thundar would change the king forever.

Chapter
2

Thundar's staff entered his chambers to find him huddled in bed, hunched under his silk sheets. He had one arm stretched out, shaking his service bell. They took caution while getting him ready. They gently fixed his hair and spoke softly, only when they had to. Even his own shadow seemed to frighten him. His servants decided they should walk softly and keep their distance; they had heard of *Thundar the Timid* before. Grizby wrote of it in great detail on page fifty-six of the list.

Grizby dispatched a whole crew to rid the castle of any creature or insect that could scare Thundar. He ordered another group to walk far in front to make sure nothing could catch him by surprise. No one wanted to be the person who sent the great king Thundar crying into a corner. It would be a long and tedious day, but the staff was up for the challenge.

The king cautiously walked the long, dimly lit corridor leading to his throne room. The flickering of the torches on the walls made him anxious, so his escorts stayed with him the whole way.

They were doing a fine job protecting him from any embarrassing displays of child-like fear. Then suddenly, footsteps echoed behind them, rapidly hitting the damp stone walkway. "Your majesty!" a voice called out, much too loud and too close for comfort.

Thundar nearly leaped right out of his majestic, silk robes. He yelped like an injured pup and dove behind the nearest servant. Grizby swiftly grabbed the intruder by his ratty collar. The boy was one of the castle's many squires. "Have you gone mad, child?" Grizby whispered to the servant. "This is not a good day for an unexpected interruption."

"I'm s-s-sorry, m'lord." the boy stuttered out. "But there's something you need to see. Quickly!"

The squire led them to the tallest guard wall of the castle and pointed out toward the horizon. Perched atop the Hill of Nema was the distinct shadowed outline of a large beast. The Hill of Nema was far away, but there was no mistaking the massive creature – it was a dragon.

They watched in frightful awe as a burst of flames spewed from the mouth of the silhouette, spraying light on the dragon's monstrous features.

Thundar the Mighty squealed in terror and fled the scene at the mere sight of a dragon. He scampered back into the sanctuary of the inner castle walls.

Grizby slowly shook his head. "A dragon. That is *really* poor timing."

Chapter 3

Some who did not know better would wonder how Thundar ever became king at all. However, he was not always so volatile. Nor did he frighten as easily as a schoolchild. He had served the kingdom of Astoria with honor and strength for many years. He repelled enemy invasions and personally fought in heroic battles.

No one claimed to know exactly why he had been shattered into so many personalities, but there were always rumors. Thundar became a child-king at the age of eleven. Some say the years of stress since that day had finally gotten to him. Others whispered about a curse laid upon him by a vengeful witch he had banished years ago.

Whatever the cause of his misfortune, he had learned to cope with it. The kingdom loved Thundar and despite his shortcomings, he served his people well. Of course, he always had a little help from Grizby. So far, the kingdom had yet to face a threat as dire as a dragon. Grizby knew he had to help the king find some courage, so he quietly made his way to Thundar's chambers. He rapped softly on the solid oak door, not wanting to spook the already shaken king.

"E-enter." Thundar muttered.

"Astoria is in desperate need of your leadership, my king." Grizby said to him as he entered. Thundar was sitting on the edge of his colossal bed. Candles flickered relentlessly from bedside tables. Their light danced around the grandness of the bedroom, and illuminated the fear on Thundar's face.

"By now," Grizby continued, "most of the kingdom will be aware of the dragon in our lands. There will be panic."

"They should panic!" the king roared and looked over his shoulder at a startled Grizby. "Let some knight or soldiers handle this task."

Grizby sat down beside the king and spoke calmly. "Your father once told me that true courage is not being *fearless*, but being afraid and still doing what must be done. If the great king of Astoria cannot rise to this challenge, then how will your people find the courage to do so in your place?"

The king thought for a moment. "You are right, Grizby. Any fool can ride into battle and swing a sword. It takes a true warrior to know which battles to fight and which to leave for another." Thundar rose from his bed and tightened his robe. "I think I am just the fool this kingdom needs!"

"That's the spirit!" Grizby clapped. "Wait, what?"

Thundar stood triumphantly next to a stunned Grizby. "Your words give me courage. I will face this dragon, alone if I must."

"That's not what I had in mind, my lord. I only meant for you to be brave enough to address your people, reassure them that the dragon will be driven from our lands." Grizby reasoned.

"Yes, well, I can do better than that. I am Thundar the Mighty, am I not?"

Chapter 4

Grizby was a tall, slender, pale skinned, orange haired scholar. He was twenty-four years old when his cousin, King Eason, named him caretaker of Thundar. When King Eason died, Thundar took the throne and Grizby stayed by his side. For the ten years since, he has abided by that title and all that it demanded. There are few in Astoria wiser, and none more loyal, than he is. Which is why Thundar knew Grizby would follow him to the Hill of Nema, whether he liked it or not.

The Kingdom of Astoria had no shortage of brave knights or loyal soldiers, but it did have a shortage of dragon slayers. It would take an especially courageous person to confront a dragon, and very few such people lived within any kingdom. Astoria had little use for such skills. After all, there had not been a dragon seen in the lands for decades. All that remained were stories passed down through the generations telling of vicious, fire-breathing, man-eating beasts.

Lance and Jory

It is no wonder only two brave souls dared to join Thundar and Grizby on that brisk, autumn morning. Jory and Lance were loyal knights from the king's personal protection brigade. Jory led the four of them, while Lance guarded the rear.

Thundar rode his steed as near to Grizby as he could. He flinched at nearly every darting insect and chirping bird that caught his attention. Then, in a brief moment of panic, Thundar threw a desperate swipe at a passing dragonfly and tumbled off his horse. Grizby rushed to help the king to his feet, while Jory and Lance tried their best not to laugh.

"I am starting to think nature will be the death of me, long before the dragon." Thundar quipped, jumping back onto his horse. "I wonder if this adventure is not a grave mistake?"

Chapter
5

The trek to the hill of Nema was less than a half-day's journey. It included a long ride through the golden wheat and barley fields outside the kingdom walls, then a trip through Vestuga Forest.

Vestuga Forest was the most dreaded place in all of Astoria. Fearless mystical creatures known as spriggans protected the woods and all that grew there. Some say that only those who were pure of heart may leave the forest after they had entered. That is why people went around, following the river, instead of going through.

Once a year, many religious pilgrims made the ominous voyage through those harsh woods to pray at the Tree of Nema. Many of them were never seen again.

Unfortunately for Thundar and his crew, going around it was not an option. That would add too much time to their trip, time they could not afford to lose.

"I am sorry gentleman, but I have bad news." Grizby said, pulling his horse to a stop. The others did the same, a few feet from the edge of the trees. "We cannot go around the forest, we must go through."

Jory laughed out loud. "That is funny. We're not on a pilgrimage, we're on a dragon hunt."

Grizby's horse was growing leery standing so close to Vestuga Forest. "Precisely. We will lose half the day going around and risk the dragon moving toward the villages." he informed them while steadying his horse. "We cannot take that chance."

Thundar trotted his horse toward the trees. "He's right. We must go through." He looked over at Jory with a sarcastic smile. "Or are you worried that you are not pure of heart?"

With a flick of their reins, Thundar and Grizby rode slowly into the forest. Lance and Jory reluctantly followed.

Chapter
6

Most people believed that because no one ever heard dragons talk, they were mindless creatures. This was not true. Simply because dragons chose not to speak to humanimals, did not mean they were not talking. And they were definitely not without thought.

The white dragon scraped its massive paws across its face. It snarled, and breathed searing flames into the mid-day sky. It moaned, then dropped abruptly to the ground, kicking up a cloud of loose dust. It was frustrated and quickly losing its patience.

It was well aware that the humanimals were getting closer. It could sense their fear and hatred, even all the way through the forest. It knew why they were coming; it had dealt with their kind before. They would always come with their swords and spears and shields. Always slicing, shouting and piercing. They had so much blind fear and misplaced anger.

But it was tired of fighting, and too weak to fly away. The white dragon's head throbbed in endless pain. It had to do something to make it stop. It had tried eating cattle, moose, trolls, piles of lettuce and carrots, even branches and tree bark. Nothing had helped.

"And yet", it thought, *"humanimals are always in good supply."* However, it knew there was a chance they would not survive the forest, and the dragon was still in great pain.

Then it had an unusual idea. The white dragon scooped up a pile of stones in its powerful jaws and began chomping. It was not long before it spit the crumbled pieces of rock into the air, with a fresh spout of flame. Then it roared a deep, billowing roar - "*nothing.*"

Vestuga was a dark and gloomy forest. It was covered by a thick canopy of leaves from tall, healthy trees. Not only was it dense with many different varieties of trees, but it was home to countless species of animals, as well. Bear, chipmunks, deer, electric vipers, even wood trolls were all said to dwell within it. Spriggans protected all of them, when needed.

Spriggans were a proud, magical race of creatures whose sole purpose was to protect the forest and all those who lived there. They took the appearance of small trees and were thus nearly impossible to find. But once they discovered a threat, they sprung to life and became fierce warriors of the woods. Rumors stated that their eyes glowed bright orange, and that they threw enchanted spears at their prey. Any creatures hit by those spears were turned into spriggans, themselves. This ensured that their ranks remained strong over the centuries.

Thundar led his men single file down a tight, winding trail. It was slow progress. The trees crowded all around them, reaching out from the shadows beyond the path. Branches were like fingers, grasping at their armor and saddle straps. The whole crew was more than a bit on edge, especially Thundar. His newfound fear of everything was reaching a breaking point.

"I do not like this. Perhaps we should turn back." Thundar whispered. He was visibly shaking.

"I agree." replied Jory and Lance, in unison. Their heads nodded vigorously as they glanced from side to side.

"We cannot." Grizby answered from behind the king. "It is too late to give in to fear. We must press on."

Thundar and Grizzby

Lance peered over his shoulder, keeping a close watch behind him, as they continued down the trail. "Why am *I* always last in line?" he quivered.

"Because you are the best sword in our group, Lance… And because *I* obviously can't be the first to go." Thundar joked, looking back at Lance with a sly smile. "Don't worry, I see a clearing up ahead. We can rest and gain our composure."

The meadow provided the first rays of sunlight the knights had seen since entering Vestuga Forest. It was a small clearing, with bright green grass, and one small tree beside a rumbling stream. It was peaceful and inviting; a direct contrast to the spooky, dark woods they traversed to get there.

Grizby sat down against the lone tree. "Let's rest here and have a bite to eat. We will need our strength when we face the dragon."

Lance sat down beside Grizby and opened up his satchel. "Sadly, all I brought for us is bread."

"Bread is better than nothing." Thundar replied, stuffing his mouth.

"Hold on, look what I caught!" shouted Jory from down the stream. He had a snake wriggling in his hands. It was pitch black, with one light blue streak down its belly; a blue streak that Jory did not notice. "Looks like we're having snake for lunch."

Thundar jumped to his feet. "Put that down, you fool! It's an…"

Suddenly, a bright flash lit up the meadow, followed by a loud *pop!* A sharp stream of energy jolted through Jory and within seconds he was on the ground.

"…electric viper." Thundar finished his warning a moment too late.

Lance and Grizby fell over laughing at the sight of Jory trying to stand back up, and then falling again. He had lines of smoke rising from his hair and arms.

"Very funny." Jory said, drawing his sword. "But we're still having snake for lunch."

The viper attempted to escape back to the water, but Jory sliced it in half with one swipe.

"What have you done, Jory?" Thundar said as he looked frantically around the woods.

"The spriggans will be after us now, for sure!" Lanced yelled as he grabbed his horse's reins. The others followed his lead. As they galloped back to their dark trail, the one small tree in the meadow began to move. "That tree was a spriggan!" Jory yelled as a spear buzzed by his head. "Gross, and you touched it, Grizby!"

Angry trees came to life all around them as they weaved through the path. Orange eyes glowed like fireballs through the darkness of the forest.

"I don't want to be a spriggan!" Lance wailed. "I look horrible in green!"

"Less panicking, more riding!" commanded Grizby.

Spriggans sprung to life all along the trail as they rode. Spears sliced through the air, each one a narrow miss.

"We're almost there. I can see the edge of the forest!" shouted Thundar.

They were only feet from escaping when a spear grazed Lance's arm. It scraped his armor, but it was enough to knock him off balance. He tumbled to the ground with a thud, and his horse continued without him.

Thundar and Jory both reared their horses around to rescue him. "Go, my lord." Jory said. "I'll get him. We'll catch up."

Jory grabbed Lance's hand and heaved him onto the back of his horse, narrowly avoiding a spriggan's spear. Within moments, freedom was in sight. Jory and Lance could see Thundar and Grizby leaving the forest not far in the distance.

"We're almost there." Jory reassured Lance, spears still zooming by their heads. Spriggans continued to emerge from the sides of the trail, even as Jory and Lance reached the edge of the forest.

Thundar and Grizby were waiting for them in a small field outside of the woods. Lance and Jory jumped from the tired horse and looked back to Vestuga Forest. They all laughed and excitedly shook hands.

"I cannot believe we made it." Jory sighed with relief.

"I know." Lance replied. "Good thing those spriggans have terrible aim!" he laughed and slapped Jory on his back.

Then, a lone spear soared through the air and slashed Jory across his right arm. This time, it did not merely scratch leather, it drew blood. Jory began to transform into a spriggan right before their eyes. He gave them all one last smile as his face turned to dry bark and his eyes morphed into orange glowing orbs. Suddenly, an unseen force pulled Jory back into Vestuga Forest. He faded out of sight, with barely a sound.

Thundar allowed a moment of silence for Jory, after which, they all exchanged fond words and memories. Once those somber minutes had passed, he clasped Lance by the arm, "We will celebrate Jory's life properly when this is all over, I promise."

Those brief moments were all the sorrowful friends had time for. The hill of Nema was looming ever closer and none of them knew when the dragon would make its move.

Chapter
8

As the riders drew closer to the base of the hill, they could hear the fierce roar of the dragon breaking through the breeze. They could see the sprites of flame dancing in the sky. At times, Thundar thought he could hear a strange moaning, as well. It sounded as if a long lost soul haunted the surrounding lands.

But they could not yet *see* the dragon. Only the top of the ancient yew tree was visible. It was the oldest and tallest tree in Astoria. Its thick branches stretched high in the sky, as if chasing the sun.

"The beast must still be waiting below the Tree of Nema." Lance said, aiming his sword toward the hill.

"You think he waits for us to come?" asked Grizby, beginning to feel quite timid, himself. "Perhaps it is only on a pilgrimage." he joked. But no one laughed with him. Their fears were beginning to take over.

"Or it knows we are coming and waits for us. What else would it be doing up there?" Lance questioned.

Thundar cleared his dry throat. He had heard enough talk of the dragon; it was making him even more uneasy. "I've never heard of a dragon that waited for an invitation to attack. Either it attacks or it does not. Whatever its purpose, it cannot stay in Astoria."

The air became hotter as they approached the base of the hill. They could hear the heavy breathing of the dragon, mixed with occasional growls and bursts of flames. Thundar realized that the strange moaning was coming from the dragon, but he did not know why. Regardless, the time had come for the timid king to face his fears and do what had to be done. Or to shrink away with shame.

Chapter 9

Thundar, Grizby, and Lance dismounted from their horses and gazed up the grassy hill. The sun was bright and the sky was nearly clear. Birds flew below the scattered wisps of afternoon clouds. It would have been a welcomed moment of peace were it not for the fire-breathing dragon lurking at the top.

"Well, my Lord," Grizby began, "it seems the time is at hand. We'll be behind you the whole way."

Thundar looked fearfully at Grizby. "So I'm to go first, then?" he quivered.

Lance nervously shook Thundar's hand. "Yes, this time I do not mind going last, my lord."

Grizby cleared his throat and chuckled. "As I said, we'll be right behind you."

When Thundar reached the top of the hill, he could finally see the dragon. Even lying under the great tree, it was immense. Its bright white scales shimmered in brief patches of sunlight. It had a long tail that curved along beside it, lined with four spikes at the tip. Its massive bottom jaw had several teeth jutting up from behind its lip. It was a beautiful and terrifying creature, the likes of which Thundar had never seen.

Just as Grizby and Lance peaked over the edge of the hill, the dragon lifted its head and spewed forth a startling roar. It followed that with a wide stream of orange flame. All of them yelped in fright.

The dragon, now aware of their presence, rose to its feet and lumbered toward them. Its head swayed menacingly as it walked. Its steps shook the ground around them. As it reached nearer, its wings flapped away from its spiny back, forcing out blasts of hot air. The three brave knights, now as one, drew their swords.

"It looks grumpy." whispered Lance.

"*So am I.*" replied Thundar.

Just as swiftly as they spoke the words, the monster was on them. Before they could blink, it swiped up Grizby with its huge, four-fingered claw, and tossed him aside like a dog's chew toy. Then it slapped Lance away, sending him tumbling down the hill.

Thundar's first instinct was to run. He wanted to run hard and far and not look back. He was so afraid, he could barely grip his mighty broadsword. He was shaking and sweating and began to worry that the dragon would notice his fear.

Pull it together, you fool! he thought.

Thundar felt more afraid than he ever had before. But in that moment, he felt an emotion even stronger than his fear - *shame*. He felt ashamed that he had the urge to run and leave his friends to their fate. He had to be better than that. Somehow, he had to be *Thundar the Mighty*.

Chapter 10

Thundar stood his ground and stared into the fiery face of the white dragon. It was visibly angry as it opened its wide jaws, ready to incinerate him in an instant. But Thundar did not want to be a dragon's dinner. He did not come all this way, facing his crippling fear, only to die without a fight. He pulled back and slapped the cranky dragon across its face. A collection of spit and one pointy dragon's tooth popped from its mouth. The tooth bounced on the ground beside them.

Grizby, watching from a safe distance, could not believe what he had witnessed. Did Thundar the Timid really just *slap* a fire- breathing dragon across the face?

The white dragon staggered backward, rubbing its jaw. The two enemies both looked at the tooth, then back at each other.

"Oh boy." Thundar said, quickly regretting his decision.

The dragon peered at Thundar with eyes that could pierce armor, and lifted up on its back legs. It lunged at him, chomping with its powerful jaws, but it bit nothing but air. Thundar dodged the attack with a roll to his right and readied his sword.

He gathered his courage and stabbed at the white beast, but missed. He stumbled forward, right into the dragon's clutches. It swiped him up with its strong claw and lifted him to its face. *This is it.* thought Thundar. *I am going to die with the taste of this dragon's rancid breath in my mouth!*

Just when Thundar readied his sword for one final, desperate strike, the dragon did something unexpected. It wiggled its jaw, and then spoke. "Today is your lucky day, king of the humanimals." it said quietly, in a strong, raspy tone.

"You… you can speak?" Thundar replied, shocked at the revelation.

The dragon smiled. "Of course we can speak. But let's keep that between us.", it said. "You have unwittingly done me a service, so I will return the favor and leave your kingdom."

The white dragon dropped Thundar to the ground. Without another growl or spent flame, it lifted into the sky and soared away. Thundar stood in silence, still slightly trembling with fear. Lance wobbled to his side as Grizby picked up the dragon's tooth.

"Are you alright, my lord?" Lance asked, out of breath. "What in the world did you do to it?"

"Dental work." said Grizby, holding up a large, blackened tooth. "The dragon must have been in pain from this rotten tooth. That's why he was moaning."

Thundar examined the tooth closely. "He really *was* just a grumpy old dragon."

"Yes. In terrible need of a dentist." Grizby remarked, with a wide smile. They all shared a hearty laugh and plopped down at the base of the ancient tree. "For a moment, it looked as if you and the dragon were having a conversation." he continued and nudged Thundar in the arm.

"Do not be foolish, Grizby, dragons cannot speak. I was merely begging for my life!" Thundar joked with them.

"I only wish Jory had made it." Lance added. "He would have enjoyed watching you slap a dragon."

They sat silently for a moment, reflecting on the hardships of their journey. And they fondly remembered the hero they lost along the way.

Thundar had the urge to toss the tooth away with a good heave, but Grizby grabbed his arm. "I'd like to keep that, my lord, if I may. It will serve as a lasting reminder." Thundar smirked,

"A reminder of what, the day I became Thundar the Dentist?

"For a moment, the companions roared their billowing barbarian laughter. Then a large spider fell from the tree and plopped onto Thundar's lap. The brave, dragon-slapping king sprung to his feet and hollered, "Get it off!" He rushed frantically down the hill while Grizby and Lance watched with wide eyes.

And their great barbarian laughter began again.

The End

The Children's Dictionary of the R.U.M.P. Chronicles

<u>Unpredictable</u> – Something difficult or impossible to know beforehand.

<u>Arachnaphobic</u> – Having a strong fear of spiders.

<u>Prosperous</u> – Having continued success.

<u>Personality</u> – The different thoughts, feelings, and behaviors that make you unique.

<u>Anxious</u> – Having uneasy or nervous feelings.

<u>Silhouette</u> – A dark, shadowy outline caused by light behind an object.

<u>Sanctuary</u> – A place of safety or protection.

<u>Volatile</u> – Changing often and unexpectedly.

<u>Vengeful</u> – Wanting to get revenge on someone for something they did.

<u>Dire</u> – Terrible; or extremely urgent.

<u>Illuminated</u> – To bring into the light; or to make something understood.

<u>Abided</u> – Lasted or continued on.

<u>Quipped</u> – Said something funny and/or smart.

<u>Ominous</u> – Showing a sign of something bad to come.

<u>Pilgrimage</u> – A journey to a holy place.

<u>Precisely</u> – Very exact.

Humanimals – A term used by dragons and other creatures to refer to humans.

Billowing – To rise or swell outward.

Varieties – Having different forms or types.

Vigorously – Done with force or energy.

Composure – Calmness of mind and/or behavior.

Traversed – To pass through, across, or over.

Wriggling – To twist and turn like a worm.

Reared – To rise up on the hind legs.

Somber – Dark and gloomy.

Looming – Coming closer; uncomfortably near.

Dismount(ed) – To get down from something.

Jutting – Sticking out, up, or forward.

Lumbered – Moved with heavy steps; slow, heavy approach.

Menacingly – Showing negative intentions.

Rancid – A strongly unpleasant smell or taste.

Revelation – Something that is revealed; the act of making something known.

Unwittingly – Doing something where the result is accidental or unintentional.

Frantically – Being done in a wild, hurried way.

Thanks for reading Thundar the Mighty!
If you enjoyed this book,
don't forget to leave a review.

Also from Savage Owl Press:

The Three Little Kittens
The Three Little Pigs
This is a Poetry Book
All These Broken Bones
Much Too Much
Silly Moon
And more coming soon!

www.ingramcontent.com/pod-product-compliance
Lightning Source LLC
Chambersburg PA
CBHW071721140626
46557CB00012B/1191